Original story by Alain Grée, illustrated by Luis Camps
Translated by Linda B. Booth

Ronnie the Rabbit

Frog Pond Friends

Derrydale Books, New York

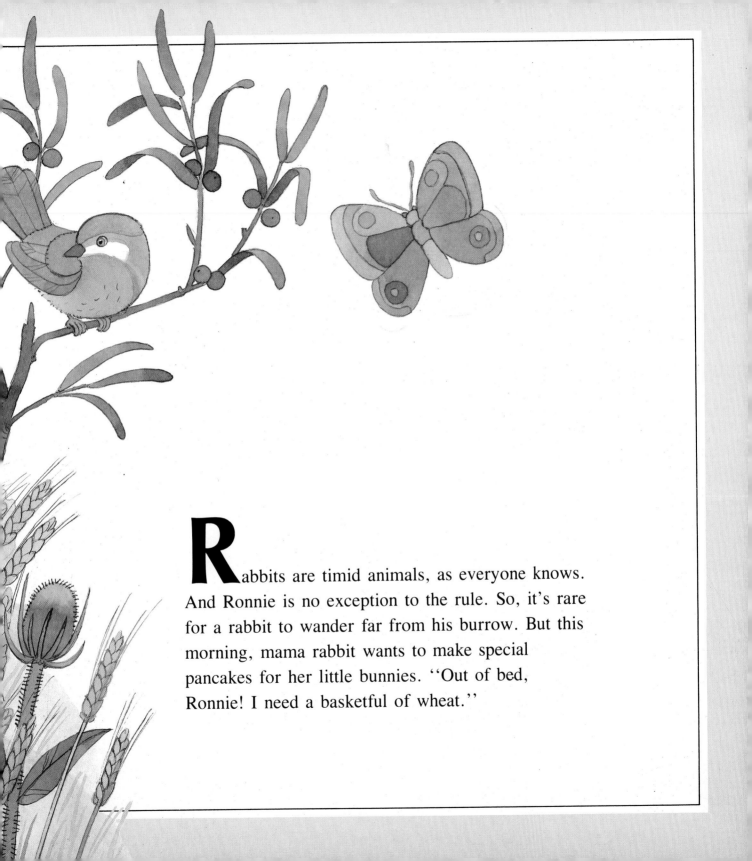

Rabbits are timid animals, as everyone knows. And Ronnie is no exception to the rule. So, it's rare for a rabbit to wander far from his burrow. But this morning, mama rabbit wants to make special pancakes for her little bunnies. "Out of bed, Ronnie! I need a basketful of wheat."

And so, since daybreak, our friend has been in the fields at the edge of the woods, gathering stalks of wheat. The sky was bright, the sun pleasant and the grain had never been more golden. All is well up till now, but on the way back home, he hears Sammy the squirrel shouting excitedly from atop the blue spruce:

"Watch out, Ronnie! I see Felix prowling in the bushes. I wouldn't dawdle if I were you—he's promised to catch you."

Felix the fox! Rabbits don't have a worse enemy.

Better scurry home . . .
"Be careful," warns
Benjamin the beaver. "Felix
is waiting at the entrance of
your burrow."
"Ronnie, I'll hold him off so
you can reach your family,"
Barbie the bee offers. She
isn't very big, but her sting
can really hurt.

Foxes hate being stung. While a sorry Felix nurses his
wounded paw, Ronnie runs home at full speed. But, oh,
what a sad sight awaits him at his burrow.
"I would have barricaded the door," explains Benjamin,
"but that nasty fox swept through here in a second."
"I tried to block the entrance with my shell," adds
Charlotte the turtle, "but that didn't stop him."

Ronnie's heart was beating like a drum. His wife is all alone at home with their three little ones! What if that ferocious fox has found them? Luckily for the family, Ronnie built the burrow like a puzzling maze. Dozens of zig-zagging tunnels and false exits criss-cross underground. Not only hasn't Felix found his way to the family, the Frog Pond Friends help him get hopelessly lost. . . .

I'm stuck!

Felix, you're getting hot!

Felix, where are you?

Confused by the shouts from above, the fox goes around
and around in circles, while Ronnie slips back home
unnoticed. How wonderful to find his family safe and
sound!

"Nobody knows how to dig a better burrow, nor find
finer wheat than you," Norma praised. "Felix will never
find our hiding place!"

Nevertheless, Ronnie still felt uneasy. Felix, like all foxes, is very cunning. "If he finds us, we'll be trapped. I'm going to build an escape tunnel quickly."

In a minute he made a new map and collected his tools.

From down below he hacked away at a new tunnel. . .

digging toward the bright blue sky. . . . .

He dug out each and every rock with an axe. . .

and carried away buckets of stone and sand.
What a worker!

"Hurry!" Norma cries suddenly. "I hear Felix!" Too late—the fox's snout pokes out from the last turn in the tunnel.

"It's true," mutters Felix, "your hiding place is impossible to find. But look! Lucky for me, during his escape, Ronnie dropped some wheat behind him. I'll just follow the trail."

"Look at the kernels of wheat!" exclaims Sammy, outside. "They lead straight to the burrow!"

"If we don't do something," adds Benjamin, "Felix will make fast work of the rabbit family." Harry the hedgehog has an idea. "If I roll down the new tunnel Ronnie just dug, I can block the entrance to their home." With a ball of spikes at the entrance, Felix comes to a prickly dead end.

"Hooray for Harry!" cry the Frog Pond Friends joyously. "They're saved!"

The fox has such bad memories of this adventure that to this day he makes a mile detour around any hedgehog. And Ronnie and Norma's little ones have picked their "guardian angel" as a playmate. So Felix is sure never to lurk near the burrow again. Remember the saying: if you strike, you get stung!

Till we meet again, Frog Pond Friends!

RABBITS
MORE ABOUT THEM

Timid and quiet, rabbits prefer not to go out in the daytime. Fearing attack by foxes, badgers and wild boars, they rarely leave their shelter before dark. In winter, rabbits must nibble bark and tree roots. But in the summer their meals include wheat, corn, clover, sugar beets and cabbage. Unfortunately, rabbits do such damage to gardens and farmland that they have reason to fear shotguns as much as a fox's bite.

Woe to the long-eared rabbit caught far from his burrow. Only his speed can possibly save him from his enemies. It's easier for rabbits to protect themselves underground.

Rabbits dig a network of tunnels with numerous exits in the burrow where they live with their families. Females make special fur-lined nests for their young and feed them their milk. Blind for the first two weeks, the little bunnies can take care of themselves a month after they are born.

Good luck, rabbit friends!

Printed in Spain